ERK!

"Annie!" my mother called. "Breakfast!"

"Be there in a minute!" I yelled from my walk-in closet. I was looking for a cardboard crown for play tryouts. I dropped to my knees and gave my sleeping bag a shove.

"*Erk!*" a voice said. A small, scratchy voice, coming from the floor. It sounded like my old talking doll.

I reached under the sleeping bag. My hand touched something smooth and warm. It felt like an arm. Or a leg. A real one!

*Some*thing was in the closet, but what? Suddenly, the sleeping bag moved. A soccer ball came rolling toward me. A pile of clothes flew into the air. And then I could see . . .

THERE'S A TROLL IN MY CLOSET

by Carol Ellis

Illustrated by Pat Porter

A BYRON PREISS BOOK

A MINSTREL® BOOK

PUBLISHED BY POCKET BOOKS

New York   London   Toronto   Sydney   Tokyo   Singapore

A MINSTREL PAPERBACK *ORIGINAL*

A Minstrel Book published by
POCKET BOOKS, a division of Simon & Schuster Inc.
1230 Avenue of the Americas, New York, NY 10020

Copyright © 1994 by Byron Preiss Visual Publications, Inc.
Cover artwork copyright © 1994 by Ted Enik.

Special thanks to Ruth Ashby.

Developed by Byron Preiss
Executive Editor: Wendy Wax
Editorial Assistant: Vicky Rauhofer
Illustrations by Pat Porter
Typesetting by Jackson Typesetting Company

ISBN: 0-671-87161-7

First Minstrel Books printing January 1994

10 9 8 7 6 5 4 3 2 1

A MINSTREL BOOK and colophon are registered
trademarks of Simon & Schuster Inc.

Printed in the U.S.A.

CHAPTER 1

WHAT'S A TULA?

It was seven-thirty Monday morning.

"Annie!" my mother called from the kitchen. "Are you dressed yet?"

"Yes!" I called back. "I just need to find something in my closet!"

Mom laughed. "Good luck!"

I *was* going to need some luck. My closet is a disaster area.

Usually, I don't mind the mess. But that day my third-grade class was having tryouts for the play we'd written. I was dying to get the part of the princess. I knew I didn't look very princess-like. I have plain brown eyes and plain brown hair just long enough for a short ponytail.

But I also had a cardboard crown covered with aluminum foil. If I wore it for the tryouts,

1

maybe it would help me get the part. There was just one problem—it was in the closet.

My closet is the big, walk-in kind. It has shelves on one side for toys and books, and a rod on the other for clothes. There's an aisle in the middle that's always filled with soccer balls and stuffed animals, sneakers and piles of dirty clothes.

I opened the closet door and kicked some shoes out of the way. I stepped inside and looked up at the toy shelves. No crown.

"Annie!" my mother called. "Breakfast!"

"Be there in a minute!" I yelled. I dropped to my knees and gave my sleeping bag a shove.

"Erk," a voice said. A small scratchy voice, coming from the floor. It sounded like my old talking doll.

I reached under the sleeping bag. My hand touched something smooth and warm. It felt like an arm. Or a leg. A real one! I almost got scared. Then I decided it was my little brother, Bobby. He's two and likes to hide in the closet. I squeezed the arm or the leg and pulled.

Whatever was in my hand pulled back. I pulled again. Then I heard Bobby giggle. But he was giggling in the *kitchen.*

I jerked my hand away so fast, I fell backward. Now I was scared for real. *Some*thing was in the closet, but what? Suddenly the sleeping bag moved. A soccer ball came rolling at me. A pile of clothes flew into the air. And then I could see.

I know this is hard to believe, but what I saw was a creature. That's all I could think to call it. A creature with a round, tan face, green eyes, a flat nose, and chipmunk cheeks. My crown was hanging from one of its ears. Its hair stood almost straight up from its head. The hair was long and shaggy. And bright pink.

My heart was pounding. I started scooting backward.

"Wait!" the creature cried, scrambling up. It was wearing something purple and shimmery, sort of like a big T-shirt. Its feet were bare. Each one had four stubby toes. Each hand had four stubby fingers. The stumpiest one could have been a thumb.

The creature wasn't much bigger than my little brother. But I wanted something between us, so I grabbed my giant teddy bear and held it in front of me. The creature jumped back.

"Brown bear," it said. "Mammal. Feeds largely on fruits and insects, but also on flesh. Have a nice day!"

Then the creature closed its eyes, snapped its fingers, and said, *"Shamat-Shamaz."*

3

I didn't know what to expect. Would it disappear? Would the bear? Would *I?*

Nobody disappeared.

The creature opened its eyes and looked around. Its face wrinkled like a raisin. I guess it was frowning. It snapped its fingers and said the weird words again. Still nothing.

"Nerks!" the creature muttered. It looked at the bear. "I think I am in a mountain of trouble," it said.

I could tell it was more scared than I was. "It's okay," I said. I couldn't believe I was talking to it. "This is just a stuffed bear."

"Stuffed with what?" it asked. "Please explain."

"I don't know what's in it. But it's not a real bear," I said. "It's a toy."

"Toy. A novelty. A plaything." The creature took the bear from me and looked at it carefully. "Made in Indonesia," it read from the label sticking out of the bear's leg. It poked at the bear. Then its mouth stretched from ear to ear, and it made a sound like squeaky bedsprings. I decided it was laughing.

I wasn't scared anymore, but I didn't know what to do. I mean, it's not often that you find a creature in your closet. I was just standing there staring at it when suddenly my mother came into the room.

"Annie, for heaven's sake," Mom said. "What's taking you so long?" She came over to the closet door.

I stood up and took a step backward. "Mom?" I said. I pointed into the closet. "You won't believe this, but look!"

My mother frowned. "I believe it, all right. It's a mess," she said. "No wonder you can never find anything. Now come eat some breakfast, or you'll be late for school."

I watched her walk out of the bedroom. She hadn't seen the creature. Had I imagined it? I hunched up my shoulders. I slowly turned my head and looked into the closet.

"How do you do?" said the creature. Its hair was still pink. It was still grinning. It was still *there*.

"I didn't imagine it," I whispered.

"Imagine. To picture in the mind," it said. "Imagine what?"

"You," I said.

The creature laughed its squeaky-bedspring laugh. "No, you didn't imagine me," it said. "How do you do? I am Tula."

"Tula?" I said.

It nodded. Its pink hair flopped. My crown fell off its ear.

"What's a Tula?" I asked.

"Tula is a name," it said. "A girl's name."

5

"Okay," I said. "A girl *what?*"

"A girl troll."

"Troll?" I said. "Did you say *troll?*"

The pink hair flopped again as Tula nodded.

"Get real," I told it.

"I *am* real!" Tula cried. Laughing, she jumped over the stuff on the closet floor and ran into my bedroom.

"Hey, wait a second!" I yelled.

"Annie Gibson!" my mother shouted. "If you're on the phone, hang up and come eat!"

I raced for the bedroom door. "Just a minute, Mom!" I called. I slammed the door and stood against it, staring at Tula. "If you're so real, why didn't my mother see you?" I whispered.

"I didn't want her to," Tula said. "I have heard that large humans often pass away when they see trolls."

I giggled. "I think you mean 'pass out,' " I said. "But, anyway, can you really become invisible if you want to?"

"Yes. Just like that." Tula snapped her fingers, but she didn't say the funny words this time. She didn't disappear, either.

"I can still see you," I told her.

"Of course," Tula said. "The first human to see a troll will always see it. And you will be the only one to hear me, too, unless I decide to become visible to others. Do you grab it now?"

" 'Get it,' " I said. "I think I do. Sort of."

"I have always wanted to see the human world," Tula said. She put my fuzzy bedroom slippers on her hands. Then she shook them off. "Trolls who have visited tell strange and wonderful tales about it. Only adult trolls are allowed to come. But I couldn't wait."

"You mean you sneaked out?" I asked.

"Yes, I used the magic words, and here I am!" Tula laughed. Then she saw the box on my bedside table. When she opened it, the music from *The Nutcracker* played. She held the box upside down and shook it.

"It's a music box," I told her. "Nothing comes out but sound. I thought you said trolls have been here before."

"I did. But not very many. And they stayed for a short time," Tula said. "So I have a lot to learn."

"You can say that again."

"I have a lot to learn," Tula said.

"No, I meant . . . never mind," I said. "Listen, if you sneaked out, aren't you going to get in trouble?"

Tula shook her head. "Time is different in the land of the trolls. I will be back before they miss me, I hope."

"How *do* you go back and forth?" I asked.

"To become invisible, I snap my fingers,"

Tula said. "To return to my world, I snap and say *Shamat-Shamaz*."

"But that's what you did when you saw the bear," I said. "And you didn't go anywhere."

"I know. I may have mixed the letters up," Tula said. "But I have plenty of time to get it right."

"Annie!" I heard my mother call. "It's now or never."

"Coming, Mom!" I shouted through the door. I got my crown from the closet floor and grabbed my bookbag. "I have to go to school," I said to Tula.

"Excellent. I'll come with you." Tula grinned. "I have a lot to learn."

"I don't know, Tula," I said. "I'm not sure my school is ready for a pink-haired troll."

"Don't worry. It will be a slice of pie," Tula said. "I'll just stay invisible."

Tula snapped her fingers. Before I could argue with her, my bedroom door opened. My little brother was standing there with a banana in his hand.

When Bobby's scared, he shrieks. And that's what he did. He pointed the banana and started shrieking.

The banana was aimed right at Tula.

CHAPTER 2

TAG-ALONG TULA

Bobby dropped the banana. Tula picked it up and looked at it. "*Banana*, correct?" she said.

"Right," I said. "Bobby, be quiet!"

"Tropical fruit. Mmm!" Tula said. She peeled the banana and took a bite. This made Bobby shriek even louder.

"Annie?" my mother called. "What's going on?"

"Nothing, Mom!" I shouted. "Bobby just dropped something." I heard my mother's footsteps, and I knew she was coming to see what was wrong.

"My little brother can see you!" I said to Tula. "And my mother will, too. Do something, quick!"

"*Nerks*," Tula said. Actually she mumbled, because her mouth was full. She handed me the rest of the banana and snapped her fingers.

I knew she'd really disappeared this time, because Bobby stopped screaming and blinked his eyes. He looked totally confused.

"It's okay, Bobby," I said. I gave him back the banana just as my mother came down the hall.

Bobby stared at the banana. Then he stared at the spot where he'd seen Tula. He didn't scream, but he started to whimper.

"What's the matter?" my mother asked him.

Bobby didn't even try to tell her. I said the first thing I could think of. "I think he wants my crown," I told her, holding it out. "I'm going to use it at the tryouts, remember?"

"Oh, the crown!" my mother said. "Well, Bobby, Annie needs that crown today. But you have one from Burger King in your room. Come on, let's go get it."

Mom took Bobby's hand and led him to his room. I looked at Tula. "Let's get out of here," I whispered.

"I'm glad he wasn't the first human to see me," Tula said as we went into the kitchen. "He has a large voice for such a small human."

"You can say that again."

"He has a large voice—"

"No. 'You can say that again' means 'That's right,' " I explained. "It means 'I agree with you.' You don't really have to say it again." I grabbed some toast and handed Tula a piece.

11

"What happened, anyway?" I asked. "How come Bobby could see you?"

"I am not sure," Tula said. "But troll magic takes practice."

"You mean you goof sometimes?"

"*Goof.* Blunder. Botch. Bungle," Tula said. "Yes. I may goof from time to time."

"*Nerks,*" I said in troll talk. "Well, just don't bungle your magic at school, okay?"

"Don't worry. It's under control now." Tula took a bite of toast and smiled. "Nice and crunchy," she said. She gobbled the rest down.

"Okay, let's go," I said. "Mom? I'm leaving!" I yelled.

"Bye, Annie!" Mom yelled back. "Good luck at the tryouts!"

"Thanks!" I took my lunch from the counter and stuffed it into my bookbag. Then Tula and I went outside. The autumn air was cool, and there was a slight wind.

My school is only four blocks from my house. When Tula and I got to the sidewalk, I stared at everybody I saw, to make sure they didn't see Tula. Nobody yelled or pointed or "passed away," and I started to relax.

When we got in front of the house next door, Ralph, the Watsons' Saint Bernard, came running over to the fence.

"*Erk!*" Tula said when she saw him.

12

"Don't worry," I said. "Ralph's really a nice dog."

"Dog?" Tula said. "We have dogs in the land of the trolls, too. But I have never seen one this big."

Usually Ralph is very friendly. But not that morning. He didn't wag his tail and whine for me to pet him through the fence as he usually does. Instead, he growled, real deep in his throat. Then he barked. It sounded like thunder.

"*Erk!*" Tula said again. "This is man's best friend?"

At first I didn't understand why he was barking. But then I did. "Ralph sees you," I said to Tula. "You just goofed again."

"Not true," she said. "I forgot to tell you—animals can always sees trolls."

"Oh, great." Ralph was running along the fence, still growling and barking. "It's okay, Ralph," I said. "She's a friend. She just looks a little different, that's all."

I don't think Ralph believed me, because he barked even louder.

Tula stopped walking. Then she pointed a finger at Ralph and said, "*Zerbut!*"

Ralph sat down, lifted his head, and howled, just like a wolf. The sound was worse than his barking. "Come on," I said to Tula. "Let's get out of here before Mr. Watson comes out to see what's wrong."

Tula and I ran to the end of the block. We could still hear Ralph howling as we crossed the street.

I looked at Tula. "Is there anything else that can always see you?" I asked.

She shook her head. "Just you and animals. That's all."

"I hope so," I said. As we started down the next block, I tripped on a crack in the sidewalk and dropped my crown. When I picked it up, Tula pointed at it.

"What is that crown for?" she asked. "I've never heard that humans wear crowns to school."

I laughed. "They don't. Our class wrote a play—you know, a story that you act out?"

Tula nodded. "Trolls have plays, also. I have never been in one, though."

"Well, anyway, there's a princess in our play," I said. "And I'd really like to get the part. So I decided to wear the crown when we try out today."

Tula looked interested. "Tell me the story," she said.

"Well, it's about this princess who wakes up one morning and discovers that her kingdom is under a spell," I said. "Everybody's real grouchy and complaining about everything. They think

14

it's the princess's fault. But what really happened is a witch stole the princess's crown. The witch wants to take over the kingdom."

Just then, a man with a briefcase came walking toward us. He gave me a really funny look. I guess he thought I was talking to myself.

"What happens?" Tula asked. "Does the princess get the crown back?"

I nodded. The man stared at me.

"How?" Tula asked.

"She beats the witch in a riddle contest," I said. I tried to say it without moving my lips. But the man heard and gave me another weird look. I wished I could explain. But how can you explain that you're talking to an invisible troll? I just smiled at him and kept walking.

"Where was I?" I asked when the man finally got into his car.

"The princess wins a riddle contest," Tula said.

"Oh, right. There's this troll—"

"A troll!" Tula stopped walking. "There's a troll in your play?" She was really excited.

"Yes." I laughed. "Hey, now that I know what a real troll looks like, I should tell my teacher what kind of costume and make-up we'll need." Then I decided I'd better not. Ms. Monroe would ask me how I knew, and she'd never believe me if I told her. "Anyway," I said, "the troll in the play tells the princess that the witch stole the crown. But when the witch was running away with it, she dropped it, and the troll took it. And the troll will only give it to whoever wins a riddle contest. He's not a nice troll."

Tula's face wrinkled up, and she shook her head. "There *are* trolls like that," she said with a sigh. "But most of us are good."

"Well, most humans are, too," I said. "Anyway, the troll asks a bunch of riddles and the princess wins and gets the crown back and everybody's happy. Except the witch."

"What happens to the troll?" Tula asked.

"I don't know," I said. "I guess he just goes back under his rock."

"Rock! You think trolls live under rocks?" Tula said.

"We just made it up," I said. "Where *do* trolls live?"

"In the forests and hills," Tula told me. "And we sleep in caves. Big ones, with soft moss for beds." She shook her head again. "Rocks," she muttered.

"How were we supposed to know?" I asked.

"I guess you couldn't know," she admitted. "Never mind, you got something right. Trolls love riddles."

"They do? Ask me some."

Tula thought a second. Then she said, "How do you spell *trouble* with only two letters?"

"Umm . . ." I shook my head. "I don't know."

"*NV.*" Tula grinned. "Do you grab it? *Envy!*"

" 'Get it,' " I said. "Right. Ask me another one."

"What do you have when you point a finger at someone else?" Tula asked.

"Hey, I know this one!" I said. "My mom said it once when Bobby and I made a mess in the kitchen and I tried to blame it all on him. The answer is: You've got three fingers pointing right back at yourself!"

"Two fingers," Tula said.

"Oh, right." I'd forgotten—trolls only have three fingers and a thumb to begin with. "Okay, two for trolls, three for humans. Now I'll ask you a riddle from the play," I said. "How can you make a troll move without touching him?"

Tula frowned. "You could pretend to be an ogre," she said. "Ogres are our enemies. *They* live under rocks. But not all trolls would run from them."

"I'll give you the answer," I said. "My best friend, Sarah, made it up. She's good at stuff like that. The answer is: You take away the letter *T* and you make a troll roll. Get it?"

Tula laughed. "That's a good one!" she said.

"I'll tell it to everyone when I go back. I would like to meet your friend Sarah."

"Yeah, well ..." I said. I was dying to tell Sarah about Tula. But I wasn't sure how or when to do it. "Maybe you will," I said. "Sometime."

We were half a block from school now. "Listen, Tula," I said. "There aren't any extra desks in my classroom. But there's a reading corner and a science table. Nobody'll be there for a while, because we have math first thing in the morning. So you can sit in one of those places, okay?"

"Reading corner. Science table," Tula said. "Okay."

"And stay invisible," I warned her.

"It will be a slice of pie," she said.

" 'Cake,' " I told her. "A piece of cake."

Tula nodded. "Piece of cake," she said to herself.

I hoped she was right. I took a deep breath. "Okay, Tula," I said. "Time for school."

CHAPTER 3

THE PINK-HAIRED GHOST

When we walked into the classroom, I nodded my head toward the reading corner, and Tula went over to it. Then I went to my desk, which is next to Sarah's. She has curly red hair, blue eyes, and lots of freckles. When she saw me, she smiled.

"Hi, Annie," she said. "Oh, good, you found your crown. Where was it?"

"In my closet," I told her. Hanging from a troll's ear. I didn't tell her. "You can wear it when you try out, too," I said.

"Thanks," Sarah said. "I don't really care what part I get, though. I had the most fun writing the play. I hope you get to be the princess."

"Ha." Jason, who sits on the other side of me, laughed. "With a crown like that, Annie'll probably get the part of the witch."

"Very funny," I told him. I looked over at Tula.

20

There's a rocking chair in the reading corner, and she was sitting in it. If anybody else looked, they'd think the chair was rocking by itself. I waved at her to stop. She waved back at me. So did Maria, who sits near the reading corner.

"Hey, look," Sam said. He sits behind me. "There's a ghost in the rocking chair."

Tula was still rocking. Ms. Monroe hadn't come in yet, so I got up and went over to the reading corner. While I pretended to look for a book, I whispered, "Stop rocking! You're invisible, but the chair isn't."

Tula scooted off the chair and sat on the floor. "Sorry," she whispered.

I was going back to my desk when Kelly came in. Kelly looks the way a lot of storybook princesses look. She has long, dark, wavy hair and great big blue eyes. And she looked even more like a princess that morning because she was wearing a crown. A real crown with sparkly stones.

"Ooh! It's Princess Kelly!" Jason said. Then he cackled.

"Maybe *you* should be the witch," Sarah told him.

Our teacher, Ms. Monroe, came in behind Kelly. When she saw the sparkly crown, she said, "That's a beautiful crown, Kelly."

"Thanks," Kelly said. She took the crown off and turned it around in her hands. "Only it's not a crown, it's a tiara." Kelly always likes to show off. "It belongs to my mother. It's made out of rhinestones, but they look like diamonds. I figured whoever gets the part of the princess can wear it and pretend it's a crown."

"That's because she figures she'll get the part," Jason whispered.

Kelly heard him and gave him a dirty look. But I thought Jason was probably right. Kelly had talked about being the princess ever since we finished writing the play.

"There are parts for everyone," Ms. Monroe said. "And they're all important." She took the crown from Kelly and put it on her desk at the front of the room. "Okay, everybody. Morning math."

While Ms. Monroe wrote five math problems on the board, I turned to the reading corner to check on Tula. She wasn't there! I looked around nervously. Then I saw her at the science table. She was sitting in one of the chairs, staring at the hamster.

I got out some paper and started to do the math. I was on the second problem when Ms. Monroe said, "Good grief, what's wrong with Harry?"

Harry is the hamster. And I knew what was wrong with him—he'd seen Tula. Harry's a very lazy hamster. Usually he just sleeps dur-

22

ing the day and plays at night. But now he was running around his cage like crazy. He jumped onto his squeaky wheel, spun around, then jumped off and tried to climb to the top of his cage.

"Maybe he's hungry," Maria said.

"No, he just hates math, like me," Jason said.

"He's gone bonkers," Sam said. "First the chair, now Harry. What's wrong with this place today?"

"I'll quiet him down," I said. I jumped up from my desk and hurried to the science table. "Go back to the reading corner," I whispered to Tula.

"But I like watching this little furry creature," Tula said.

"Yeah, but the little furry creature is acting really strange, and everybody's wondering why," I told her. "So go back to the books. And stay off the rocking chair!"

Tula sighed, but she went back over to the bookshelves. The minute she did, Harry plopped himself down and closed his eyes. He looked exhausted.

I went back to my desk. Luckily no one asked me how I quieted Harry down. Everyone was too busy working on the math problems. I finished the second and third problems and started the fourth. That's when Maria said, "Ms. Monroe? There's something funny going on in the reading corner."

I was afraid to look, but I had to. Tula was lying on her stomach on the floor, turning the pages of a book. Of course, I was the only one who could see her. Everybody else thought the book's pages were turning by themselves. Tula was turning out to be a real troublemaker.

"Hey, Ms. Monroe," Jason said. "You're always telling us that books make things come alive. But I bet this is the first time you ever saw a live book!"

"I'm telling you, weird things are happening," Sam said. "There's a spell on this place."

"It's really spooky," Maria said.

"It's the wind," I said. "I'll close the window."

I hurried over to the reading corner and snatched the book off the floor. "Sorry, but you'll just have to sit and do nothing!" I hissed at Tula.

"Nerks!" she said.

I cranked the window closed and went back to my desk. I finished the math, but I think I got most of the answers wrong because I was so busy keeping an eye on Tula. I wasn't so sure I should have let her come to school. But leaving her at home might have been worse. If she goofed and became visible, Bobby would probably go as bonkers as Harry. I wasn't sure what my mother would do. I didn't think she'd faint, but she might call the zoo.

After we handed in our math, Ms. Monroe said it was time to go to the auditorium and try out for the play.

"Finally!" Kelly said. She grabbed her crown off Ms. Monroe's desk and hurried to be the first in line. The rest of us followed.

I took my crown, too, even though it looked shabby compared to Kelly's. And I guess I was nervous about trying out, because I forgot about Tula for a minute. But she hadn't forgotten about me. She hurried out the door right by my side. Her pink hair flopped up and down as she walked.

"Listen, Tula," I whispered out of the side of my mouth. "Don't do anything in the auditorium, okay? Just stay still and listen."

Sarah turned around and looked at me. "Who are you talking to?" she asked.

"Nobody," I said quickly.

Tula laughed and poked me in the side. "Who are you calling a nobody?"

"I didn't mean it that way," I whispered.

"Huh?" Sarah said.

"Nothing," I said to Sarah. "I was just saying some lines to myself."

"Annie?" Ms. Monroe called back. "Let's keep quiet, okay? There are other classes going on, remember."

Carol Ellis

"Okay," I said. I looked at Tula and put a finger on my lips. But Tula knew she could talk all she wanted. I was the only one who could hear her when she was invisible.

"Good luck in the tryouts, Annie," she said. "I hope you get the part you want."

"I hope so, too," I said.

Sarah turned around and gave me a funny look. "That isn't a line from the play," she said.

"Annie and Sarah, quiet please," Ms. Monroe said.

I whispered to Sarah that I'd explain later. Then I frowned at Tula. She laughed her squeaky laugh and poked me in the side again.

When we got to the auditorium, Kelly waved her hand in the air so she could be the first one to try out. I was worried she'd be really good, but she wasn't. She shouted all the lines. And she kept stumbling over words, like saying "clown" when she meant "crown."

"Boy, she really stinks," Sarah whispered to me.

"*Stink*," Tula said. She was sitting behind us. "Odor, aroma, smell." She sniffed loudly. "I don't smell anything."

I turned around. "It means she's lousy," I hissed.

"I know that," Sarah said, giving me another funny look. "Annie, you're acting kind of weird. How come you keep talking to the air?"

26

"Uh . . ." I said. I couldn't think of a good answer.

"You must be really nervous," Sarah said.

"Right, that's it," I told her. "When I'm nervous, I talk to myself."

"Well, you don't have to worry about Kelly getting the part," Sarah said.

"You can say that again," Tula said behind us. "She stinks."

When Kelly finished, Ms. Monroe asked her to try the witch. The witch doesn't have many lines. Mostly she cackles. I knew Kelly didn't want to be anyone but the princess, but Ms. Monroe said we should all try different parts. So Kelly read a couple of the witch's lines, and then she cackled. I had to admit she had a great cackle.

Sarah poked my arm. "She was born for the role," she whispered.

After Kelly it was my turn. I stuck my crown on and went up on the stage. My hands shook and so did my knees. But my voice didn't. I thought I read pretty well, and I cackled okay, too. But there were a lot more people to go after me.

Sam tried the part of the troll next, and he was perfect. He waved his arms and stamped his foot a lot, just like he was supposed to. Of course, he didn't sound anything like Tula.

"I could show him a thing or two about trolls," Tula muttered.

"Don't you dare!" I warned. Sarah was going up on the stage, so she didn't hear me talking to the "air" this time.

When the tryouts were finished, Ms. Monroe said she'd tell us who got what part at the end of the day. We went back to class, and Ms. Monroe put Kelly's crown on the art supply shelf. I could tell Kelly wasn't happy. But she'd already said that whoever was the princess would get the crown. I kept my fingers crossed that it would be me.

When it was lunchtime, I stayed behind for a minute so I could give Tula half of my sandwich.

"Why can't I join the rest of you?" she asked. "I will stay invisible."

"Yeah, but the food won't," I said. "Everybody would just see a sandwich floating through the air. Stay here and don't bother Harry," I told her, pointing to the hamster. "He's still wiped out."

After lunch everybody was crowding through the cafeteria doors when somebody up front shouted, "Look out! It's not going to stop!"

I couldn't see anything, but then I heard wheels spinning down the hall toward the cafeteria. More people started shouting. The sound of the wheels got louder and louder. And then a skateboard came zooming by.

Sam, who was next to me, yelled, "It's a runaway!"

It was a runaway skateboard, all right. With a runaway troll on it. Tula was going so fast, her hair stuck straight out behind her. Her eyes were closed, she was waving her arms like mad, and her face was all scrunched up, as if she expected to crash any second.

Everybody jumped aside as the skateboard flew through the doors of the cafeteria like a rocket on wheels. Tula was heading straight for Mrs. Kupperman, the principal of our school.

"Jump!" I shouted as Tula zoomed by. But everybody was shouting, and she didn't hear me. Luckily, no one else did either.

I shut my eyes. Then I heard a loud crash. When I finally looked, Tula was sitting on the floor. She had her hand on her head, as if she was dizzy. But I knew she was okay, because she grinned at me.

Then I looked at Mrs. Kupperman. She was sprawled out on one of the lunch tables, with spaghetti and meatballs all the way down her dress.

Mrs. Kupperman was okay, too. But she wasn't grinning at anybody. When she finally

finished yelling, she told us to go out for recess. As we were walking outside, Sam said,
"Something awesomely weird is going on
around here! That skateboard was possessed."

I knew it had looked weird to everybody
else. But there was no way I could explain
what had really happened. So I said to Sam,
"That's dumb. It was just the wind again. The
main doors were open, and the wind blew the
skateboard down the hallway." I wondered
what I'd be saying if there was no wind
outside.

Tula didn't do any more "ghostly" things for
the rest of the day, but I was nervous every
time I looked at her. And I was nervous about
the play. When school was almost over, and
Ms. Monroe picked up her list of parts, I
started biting a fingernail.

"Okay," Ms. Monroe said. "Here's the cast
list." First, she read off all the small parts.
Jason got the part of the troll's guard. Sarah
and Maria and most of the others were mem-
bers of the princess's kingdom. Ms. Monroe
still hadn't said my name. I started biting another fingernail.

Then Ms. Monroe said, "Sam, I think you'll
make an excellent troll."

"Yes!" said Sam.

"An excellent *fake* troll," Tula muttered. "He jumps and yells too much."

"And Kelly, I'd like you to play the witch," Ms. Monroe said.

Kelly's mouth dropped open.

"And thank you for lending us your crown," Ms. Monroe went on. "I'm sure Annie will enjoy wearing it."

Now *my* mouth dropped open. I couldn't believe it. I'd gotten the part of the princess!

Sarah patted me on the back. So did Sam. Jason laughed and said, "Ooh! Princess Annie!" I heard Tula cheer, and when I looked back at her, she was clapping her hands.

I just sat there, feeling great. Then I heard Ms. Monroe gasp real loud. Everybody looked at her.

Ms. Monroe was staring at the back of the room. She didn't have a banana in her hand, but her face looked just the way Bobby's had looked that morning. I could tell she was going to start shrieking any second.

Tula had become visible.

CHAPTER 4

MIX-UPS

Ms. Monroe pointed first. And *then* she shrieked. She sounded just like Bobby, too.

All the kids started to look to where Ms. Monroe was pointing. All except me. I closed my eyes again, the way I had with the skateboard incident. If Ms. Monroe could see Tula, then everybody else could, too!

But just as their heads turned, I heard Tula say, *"Nerks!"* and snap her fingers. I held my breath. When nobody else screamed, I let it out again. Tula had disappeared, just in time.

Ms. Monroe stared for a few more seconds. Then she sat down hard in her chair. Her face was real white.

A bunch of kids ran up to the front of the room. "Ms. Monroe?" Maria said. She grabbed the teacher's hand and started patting it. "Ms. Monroe, are you okay?"

Ms. Monroe groaned and put her head in her hands. "I'm all right," she said.

"She doesn't look all right," Jason whispered. "I think she's going to puke."

"She probably got sick of looking at you all the time," Sarah told him.

"What happened, Ms. Monroe?" Maria said. "Did you see a ghost?"

"I knew it!" Sam said. "I just knew it. Go ahead, Annie, try telling us it was the wind."

"Try telling you what was the wind?" Jason said.

"Whatever she saw," Sam said. "All kinds of weird things have been happening, and now this. There's a ghost around here, and Ms. Monroe got to see it! Come on, Ms. Monroe. Tell us about it."

"What did it look like?" Maria asked.

Ms. Monroe looked toward the back of the room and blinked. "I thought I saw a short . . . with pink . . . and four . . ." She stopped talking and shook her head. "No, no, it's not possible."

"I bet it was an optical illusion," I said quickly. "Right, Ms. Monroe?"

Ms. Monroe still looked a little pale. "Maybe," she said. "It *has* been a long day, and I feel a headache coming on. Yes, my eyes must be playing tricks on me." She shook her head again and stood up. "All right, everybody,"

she said. "Time to go. Don't forget your homework. And remember, you should start learning your lines for the play right away. We have
to be ready a week from Friday. That doesn't
leave us much time." All the kids got their
bookbags and followed her down the hall.

I said good-bye to Sarah. She takes the bus
home. Then my invisible troll and I started
walking.

"I am sorry I scared your teacher, Annie,"
Tula said. "But I was so excited for you, I must
have become visible."

"Don't tell me trolls become visible every
time they're excited," I said.

"Sometimes, but we can learn not to. The
magic just takes practice," Tula said.

"How much practice?" I asked. I was start-
ing to wonder if Tula would ever be able to
control her magic.

"I don't know, but don't worry," Tula said.
"I will get better. Anyway, aren't you happy,
Annie? You got the part you wanted."

"I know, and I'm *really* glad," I said.

When we came to Mr. Watson's house,
Ralph wasn't in the front yard. But just as we
were almost past, he came tearing out from the
backyard, barking and growling as he had that
morning.

"Nice dog, Ralph!" I said.

I don't think Ralph heard me.

Tula stopped walking and frowned at him. "This is a pesky canine," she said. She pointed a finger at him and said, *"Zerboot!"*

Not only did Ralph not stop barking, he started running around in a circle.

"What did you say to him?" I asked.

"It's an old troll command," she said. "It means, 'Hush and be good.' "

Ralph was still barking and running. He ran faster and faster, until he was just a blur, like a dog in a cartoon.

"It didn't work," I said to Tula. "Come on, let's get going before he completely tears up Mr. Watson's yard!"

As soon as we were out of Ralph's sight, we could hear him calming down. "I don't understand why my command didn't work," Tula said. "It always works at home. Maybe I mixed the letters up. I'll try again tomorrow."

"I can't wait," I said, rolling my eyes.

When we got home, I told Tula to go straight back to my room. Mom was at the kitchen table, reading a book. The house was quiet. I decided Bobby must be taking a nap. "Guess what?" I said to Mom. "I got the part of the princess!"

"That's great, Annie!" Mom got up and

hugged me. "I'm really happy for you. Tell me all about it."

While I told her about the tryouts and about the beautiful crown I'd get to wear, I unfolded a napkin and put a huge pile of cookies on it.

"So many cookies, Annie?" my mother said. "Is Sarah coming over?"

"Uh, no," I said. "But I'm really starving."

Before she could tell me I'd ruin my dinner, I took the cookies and went back to my room.

Tula was on top of my bed, jumping up and down and spinning around. Her eyes were closed, and she kept shaking her head back and forth.

"Tula, what's wrong with you?" I said. She didn't answer. I was sure she'd said one of her troll words and mixed the letters up. Now she'd be jumping up and down forever. In my room.

I hurried over and tapped her on the shoulder. Her eyes flew open, and she grinned at me. Then I noticed she was holding my Walkman. And buried in her wild hair were the headphones.

Tula pulled the headphones off.

Looking a little dizzy she said, "WJAM. Top Forty. Rock and roll." Then she saw the cookies I was holding. "Mmm! Pancakes, correct?"

"Wrong," I said. "Oatmeal cookies. You'll like them."

Tula took one and gobbled it down. "Excellent," she said. "Much better than what you gave me at lunch. What was that?"

I giggled. "That was peanut butter," I told her. "And if you're going to stay for a while, you'd better get used to it."

"The taste of the inside was not bad," Tula said. "But the see-through stuff on the outside was hard to swallow."

"Tula!" I said. "You ate the Baggie?"

"Baggie," Tula said. Then she frowned at me. "What's a Baggie?"

"It's a little bag to pack sandwiches in, and it's made out of plastic," I told her. "You're not supposed to eat it."

"Ah. Next time I will know," Tula said, then took another cookie. She was on her fourth one when the phone rang. Mom yelled that it was Sarah. I went to my parents' room, got their cordless phone, and brought it back to my room. Tula looked curiously at the phone—especially when I said hello into the receiver.

"Hi," Sarah said. "Guess what I heard Kelly say on the bus. She said you'd better be careful with that crown because it's very valuable."

"But she told Ms. Monroe it was made out of rhinestones, not diamonds," I said.

"I know. She's probably lying. She's just mad that you got the part she wanted," Sarah said. "That's the way she is. That's why she'll make a perfect witch."

"Maybe I shouldn't wear her crown, though," I said. "I really want to, but not if she's going to make such a big deal out of it. I mean, what if some of the rhinestones fell out? Kelly would blame me."

Tula started to cough real loud. I looked at her and saw she was trying to get my attention.

"Who's that?" Sarah asked.

Sarah could hear her! Tula must have become visible. She'd goofed again. "Um ... my mom," I said to Sarah. I patted Tula on the back.

"Oh. Well, anyway," Sarah said, "I think you should go ahead and wear the crown. After all, Kelly said it was for whoever got the part. She can't take it back now, even though I know she's dying to."

"I guess I will wear it," I said. "But I hope it's not really valuable. That would make me nervous."

Tula started coughing louder than ever and waving her hands at me.

"Speaking of dying," Sarah said. "Your mother sounds like she's choking!"

"No, she's okay. She just has a cookie crumb stuck in her throat," I said. Tula kept waving her hands at me, and now she looked scared. "Listen, Sarah, I better go," I said. "I'll see you tomorrow, okay?"

After I hung up, Tula said, "Annie, I have to tell you something!"

But just then, Bobby came into my room, looking sleepy. He didn't look sleepy for long. His eyes got wide, and he pointed a fat little finger straight at Tula. I knew he was going to shriek, so I shut the door and put my hand over his mouth.

"Don't be scared, Bobby," I said to him. I looked at Tula. "He can see you!" I told her.

"I know. Sorry," she said. "Before I started listening to the Top Forty, I was trying to remember how to get home. I kept saying different commands and snapping my fingers, and I forgot that I became visible."

Bobby was trying to peel my hand away from his mouth. "Listen, Bobby," I said. "This is a friend of mine. Her name's Tula. Now be real quiet, and I bet she'll give you a cookie."

Cookie is a magic word with Bobby. He nodded his head. I took my hand away. "Quick, give him a cookie!" I said to Tula.

Tula shoved a cookie into his mouth. Bobby kept an eye on her while he ate it. When he finished chewing, he smiled. "Tuwa," he said.

"Right," I said. "Now why don't you go into the kitchen and get some milk?"

"Stay with Tuwa," he said again.

"Oh, great," I said. "Tula has to go in a minute," I told him. "Come on, let's go get some milk together." I took his hand and led him to the door. "You stay here," I said to Tula.

"But I'd like some milk, too," she said.

"I'll bring you some," I said. "Just stay invisible."

After I gave Bobby some milk, my mother asked me to take him outside to play. While I pushed him on the swing, he asked where "Tuwa" was. I told him she'd left.

When I finished playing with Bobby, I got a glass of milk and took it back to my bedroom. Tula was sitting in my beanbag chair. She had the cordless phone in her hands, and she was pushing the buttons.

"Uh-oh!" I said. I grabbed the phone and held it to my ear.

"New Scotland Yard," a voice said. "May I help you?"

I shut the phone off. "Tula! You just called England!"

"*England*," Tula said. "Part of the United Kingdom. Population, fifty-five million, six hundred and seventy thousand. Capital city, London."

"That's right, and it's thousands of miles away," I said. "When the phone bill comes, I'll be grounded for sure!"

I was trying to explain telephones and long-distance calling to Tula when my mother yelled, "Annie! Dad's home. Come tell him about the play!"

I put the phone back in my parents' room and went into the kitchen. My father hugged me. "I hear you're going to be a star, Annie," he said. "This calls for a celebration."

"How about a raise in my allowance?" I said. Maybe then I could pay for the call to Scotland Yard, I thought.

My father laughed and shook his head. "How about some ice cream cake, instead?" he said. "I picked one up on the way home from work. We'll have some for dessert."

At dinner Bobby kept saying "Tuwa!" My parents thought he was saying "Tulip," because the wallpaper in the kitchen has tulips on it. Every time he said "Tuwa!" they smiled and said, "That's right, Bobby. Those are tulips." I kept my mouth shut. I also put some carrot sticks and half my baked potato into my napkin while they weren't looking.

Finally dinner was over. My father took Bobby into the bathroom for a bath. I cleared the table, grabbed my napkin of food, and hurried to my room.

Tula was sitting on my bed, next to my bookbag. "I brought you some dinner," I said, holding out the napkin.

Tula started to take it. Then she stopped. "First things first," she said. "I have a confession to make, Annie."

I looked around the room. I thought she must have broken something. But everything looked the same. "What did you do?" I asked.

"I heard you talking to Sarah about Kelly's crown," she said. "And how careful you must be with it." While she talked, Tula unzipped my bookbag. Then she reached inside and pulled something out. A beautiful crown that sparkled as if it were made of diamonds.

Kelly's crown.

CHAPTER 5

NERKS!

"The crown!" I said. "Oh, no!"

"Oh, yes," Tula said.

"Why did you take it?" I asked. "*When* did you take it? I didn't see you do it, and I had one eye on you all day."

"I put it in your bookbag as we were getting ready to go home," she said. "I thought you would want to practice with it."

"You should have asked," I told her. "You can't just take things. Or do trolls do that?"

Tula acted insulted. "Of course not," she said. "But the crown is for whoever plays the princess, and that's you." She handed me the crown. "I am sorry, Annie. Am I in a mountain of trouble?"

"You will be if Kelly finds out," I told her. "Or rather, I will be." I looked at the crown.

"I guess I shouldn't worry so much about Kelly, though. After all, she said whoever got the part could wear it. But don't do it again, okay?"

"I won't. I vow it," Tula said. "And you can put it back tomorrow before Kelly finds out. That way she'll stay in the night about it."

"In the 'dark,'" I said. "Okay, that's what I'll do. Right now I'd better do my homework." I took my spelling list out of my bookbag and started to study it.

Tula began to eat the carrots and potato I had brought back to the room. "What are you doing?" she asked a few moments later.

"I told you. My homework," I said, showing her the list. "I have to learn how to spell these words."

"That's how humans learn words?" she asked. "By looking at them?"

"Well, sort of," I said. "How do *you* do it?"

"Like this!" Tula grabbed the spelling list and wadded it into a ball. Before I could stop her, she stuffed it into her mouth, chomped it up, and swallowed it. "Eat and learn!" she said. "That's how."

"Tula!" I said. "That might work in the land of the trolls, but not here! How am I going to pass the test now? I can't tell my teacher that a troll ate my spelling list!"

"Don't worry," Tula said, picking a soggy sliver of paper off her lip. "I can tell you the words. I just learned them, remember?"

And she did. There were ten words on the list, and she spelled them to me while I copied them on another piece of paper. After I finished studying them the human way, I decided to learn some lines from the play. Tula wanted to help. "Okay," I said. "But you have to promise not to eat the script."

Since a lot of my lines are with the troll, I asked Tula to read that part. But after a couple of minutes I noticed something very strange. "Tula!" I said. "Your face is green! You must have eaten too many cookies!"

"It's not the cookies," Tula said. "When trolls get mad, their faces turn green. And I'm mad because the troll in your play is so wicked. I told you, most trolls are good."

"Well, how were we supposed to know?" I said. "Besides, it's just pretend."

But every time Tula read a troll line, she looked like a wrinkled green apple with cotton-candy hair. I couldn't concentrate, so I decided to read the lines to myself. Just when I was repeating the second troll riddle, Bobby banged on the door.

"Not now, Bobby!" I yelled. "I'm busy."

"Tuwa there?" Bobby said through the door.

"Oh, great," I said to Tula. "Now that he's

seen you, he's never going to stop bugging me."

"*Bug,*" Tula said. "Insect, gnat, pest."

"You can't come in now!" I yelled to Bobby. "I'm doing my homework!"

Bobby banged on the door one more time. Then I heard him walk away. "Pest is right," I said to Tula. "He's a real bother sometimes."

Tula nodded. "My little brother 'bugs' me, too."

"You have a brother?"

"Of course," she said. "I have eight brothers and six sisters."

"Tula, that's *fifteen* kids!" I said. "That's a huge family."

"Not where I come from," she said. "Most troll families have at least twenty-five."

"Wow," I said. "Well, do you miss your family yet? I mean, are you getting homesick?"

"Not yet," Tula said. "I am having too cold a time here."

"Cold?" I said. "Oh. You mean 'cool.'"

"Cool," Tula said. "And that's good, because I still haven't remembered how to get back."

I wondered how long it would take her to remember. I mean, even though it was weird having her around, it was kind of fun, too. I wasn't sure how I'd feel if she got permanently stuck here. But Tula wasn't worrying about it, so I decided not to, either.

When it was time for bed, Tula decided to sleep in my closet. "It's more like my cave," she explained.

I decided that was a good idea. If she accidentally became visible, at least she'd be hidden.

The first thing I noticed the next morning was a rattling sound. It was coming from the kitchen. At first I thought my parents were having breakfast. But then I heard the shower running. That was Dad. Then I heard Mom. She was talking to Bobby. In Bobby's room.

That meant Tula was in the kitchen! I jumped out of bed and ran down the hall.

Tula was in the kitchen, all right. She had her head stuck in the refrigerator, and she was moving bottles and jars around. The bag of oatmeal cookies was on the counter. There were only three left.

"Tula!" I said. "What are you doing?"

She pulled her head out of the refrigerator. "Good morning, Annie," she said. "I have heard about these large boxes that keep things cold. I was just exploring it."

"Yeah, well, explore my room for a while, okay?" I said. "My parents and Bobby will be coming in here any second. If they see stuff moving around by itself, they'll think the house is haunted."

"You humans are so funny. You always think there are ghosts." Tula laughed and went to my room.

When Mom saw the almost-empty cookie bag, she didn't think there were ghosts. She thought *I'd* eaten them. "Annie, you know better than to eat cookies for breakfast," she said.

"I was starving," I told her. I still was, because I hadn't eaten a thing yet. I poured myself some cereal and ate it fast. Then I went back to my room.

Tula looked at my empty hands. "No toast?"

"Toast! You just ate half a bag of cookies."

"And they were delicious," she said. "For starters."

"Well, you'll have to wait until lunch for something more," I told her. "We've got to get ready to go."

After I got dressed, I put my notebooks and Kelly's crown in my bookbag. "Okay, let's go," I said to Tula. "And remember to stay out of sight."

In the kitchen Mom had just made some toast and put it on a plate in front of Bobby. Her back was turned, and as Tula and I went by, Tula swiped a piece off the plate and shoved the whole thing in her mouth. All

Bobby saw was a piece of toast floating through the air and disappearing. He pointed and laughed. He thought it was a magic trick. He was right. He just didn't know *whose* magic trick.

When we got to the house next door, Ralph came snarling up to the fence again. Tula pointed a finger at him and said, *"Zerbat!"*

Ralph shut his mouth and looked around. For a second I thought Tula had finally said the right troll command. But suddenly Ralph started barking again, worse than ever. Then he charged toward the newspaper that was in the middle of the yard, grabbed it in his mouth, and started ripping it to shreds.

"Nerks," Tula said.

We hurried to the corner. Then I stopped and looked back. Ralph had finished killing the morning paper. The Watsons' front yard looked as if it were covered with tiny, black-and-white snowflakes.

When we got to school, I hurried down the hall to my classroom. Kelly wasn't there yet. Neither was anyone else. I looked at the school clock and saw that we were ten minutes early. Usually I'm ten minutes late!

"Sit in the reading corner again," I hissed to Tula. "On the floor." Even though no one was there to see her, someone might walk in at any moment.

I went over to the art supply shelf. I held my bookbag in front of me so no one could see what I was doing. Then, as quickly as I could, I unzipped it and took out the crown.

"Annie!" Kelly said behind me. "What are you doing with my crown?"

Chapter 6

Troll Trouble

Kelly's voice made me jump, and I almost dropped the crown. When I turned around, Kelly pointed at it. "What are you doing with that?" she asked again.

"I was just going to put it back on the shelf," I told her. It was the truth. It just wasn't the whole truth.

"I can see that," Kelly said. She sure could sound sarcastic. "But you took it out of your bookbag. I saw you. What was it doing in there?"

A troll took it home for me, I wanted to say. I would have loved to see the look on Kelly's face. But she'd think I was making fun of her, and she'd get even madder. Besides, I was getting a little mad myself.

"I took it home to wear while I practiced my

lines," I said. "I didn't know you'd mind. After all, you brought it for the princess to wear."

"Yeah, Kelly," said Jason, who was just walking in. Other kids followed. "How come you're in such a twist about it? Or are you practicing being the witch?" He cackled.

Kelly frowned at him. "It's my crown, Jason," she said. "I never told Annie she could take it home."

"You never told her she couldn't, either," said Sarah, coming up behind Jason.

Just then Ms. Monroe came into the room and asked what was going on. "Kelly's worried about her stupid crown," Jason said.

Kelly frowned at him again. "I just don't want it to get lost or broken or anything," she said to Ms. Monroe.

"Well, the best way to keep your crown safe is to keep it here," Ms. Monroe said.

"But I was thinking maybe I should take it home every day," Kelly said.

"She probably wants to wear it and make everyone bow to her," Sarah whispered to me.

"If the crown stays here, then nothing can happen to it," Ms. Monroe said a bit louder. She smiled at Kelly and I could tell the discussion was over.

Kelly didn't argue, but she looked really upset. I didn't get it. If she was so worried about the crown, the classroom *was* the best place for it.

Ms. Monroe held up the shopping bag she was carrying. "A friend of mine owns a costume shop," she said. "And she lent us a bunch of things for the play." She reached into the bag and pulled out a big, black, pointy witch's hat. "This is part of your costume, Kelly."

"Perfect," Sarah whispered.

"And Sam," Ms. Monroe said, "this is for you." She reached into the bag again and took out a wig. I couldn't believe it. The hair was shorter than Tula's, but it was almost the same shade of pink.

"A wig?" Sam said. "I have to wear a wig? Everybody'll laugh."

Everybody *did* laugh, but finally Sam took the wig and put it on. Then he started yelling and jumping around the classroom, just like the troll in the play. Everybody was still laughing, but now it was because they thought Sam was such a good actor.

When I looked over at Tula in the reading corner, her face was green. "I am truly bugged," she said.

"Okay, Sam, that's enough," Ms. Monroe said. "Time for morning math."

Sam put the wig on the shelf, and I placed the crown next to it. We all went to our desks

and did the five math problems on the board. Then it was time for spelling. I thought I would get a perfect score. But I spelled *friend* wrong. I put the *e* before the *i*.

"Sorry, Annie," Tula said when she saw me frowning at her. "I must have eaten the *e* first when we were studying late last night."

After spelling, we went to the art room and worked on the set for the play. The art teacher helped us cut big trees and a castle wall out of cardboard. Then we started painting them. Tula came along. She didn't cause any problems, but she griped about the big papier-mâché rock that was going to be the troll's home. "Only worms and spiders and ogres live under rocks," she said.

"I know real trolls live in nice clean caves," I said. I was painting red tulips on the bottom of a tree trunk.

Sam looked at me strangely. "I don't think so," he said. "Trolls are so mean they like to live where it's dark and dirty."

"Ha!" Tula muttered.

After art we went to the auditorium. We got on the stage and read our lines, and Ms. Monroe told everybody where to stand and walk. Every time Sam was on the stage playing the troll, I could see Tula's face turning green out

in the front row. It bothered me so much, I
kept goofing up my lines.

Kelly was a big help. "Gee, Annie," she said.
"I hope you know your part by next Friday,
or the play's going to be a real bomb."

Now I had something besides Tula to worry
about. By the time school was over, I was in a
bad mood.

"I am sorry about the crown," Tula said as
we walked home. "And the spelling. But it
won't happen again."

No it won't, I thought to myself, because
that's the last spelling test this week. But lots
of other things happened instead. The next day
Tula said *"Zerbet!"* to Harry the hamster, and
Harry tried to dig a hole in the bottom of his
cage. Ms. Monroe thought he was having a
nervous breakdown.

The day after that, Tula went exploring at
lunch again. This time she discovered the
piano in the music room. When I went into the
room she was playing the number one song on
the Top Forty charts. With her feet.

Then Tula joined the kickball game at recess.
Jason was sure surprised when a ball came out
of nowhere and hit him in the stomach. He
was okay, but he wouldn't stop talking about
ghosts after that.

Having a troll in my life was getting to be a

real problem. And it was getting in the way of the play. Ms. Monroe had taken me aside after Thursday's rehearsal and asked me if I was sure I could handle the part. I felt like crying, but instead I told her I knew I could. I'd just have to work extra hard. If I lost the part I'd never be able to show my face in school again!

When school was finally over on Friday, Sarah and I walked outside together. "You want to come over tomorrow?" she asked.

"Maybe," I said. I looked at Tula, who was walking on my other side. "Well, maybe not."

Sarah frowned. "Are you mad at me or something?"

"No!" I said. "Why?"

"I don't know," she said. "You've just been acting kind of funny. You're real jumpy, and you keep talking to yourself."

Tula giggled. I gave her a dirty look.

"Now that I've got the part of the princess," I said to Sarah, "I'm nervous, that's all. Can you come over to my house, Saturday?"

"Okay. See you tomorrow, Annie." Sarah waved and ran to get on her bus.

"You're mad at *me*, aren't you, Annie?" Tula said as we walked home.

"I'm not exactly mad." We were passing Ralph's house, but he didn't come charging to the fence. He must have been inside. "But you heard Sarah," I said to Tula. "She thinks I've been acting funny. And I bet some of the other kids do, too. And I have to watch you all the time to make sure you don't do something wild."

"Then I will be very tame at school from now on," Tula promised. "And I will keep my lips locked, too. But why don't you introduce me to Sarah?"

"Maybe I will," I said. "Tomorrow."

But that night Sarah called. She couldn't come over after all. Her family was going to her grandparents' for the day.

It was just as well. Tula couldn't seem to stop causing problems. She got up early Saturday morning and went into the den. The sound of Saturday morning cartoons woke everybody up. Guess who got blamed for turning the TV on too loud?

On Sunday morning Tula ate another bag of cookies and a bag of potato chips. Guess who got blamed for leaving crumbs all over the counter?

And then there was the bath.

I'm not sure how it happened.

It was Sunday night. I'd been helping Mom and Dad clean up the basement. When I came upstairs, I heard Tula singing. Then I heard Bobby laughing. And both voices were coming from the bathroom!

I ran to the bathroom and opened the door.

It was a disaster. Bubble bath had foamed out of the tub, all over the floor, and all the way up to the ceiling. All I could see was a wall of floating bubbles.

"Bobby!" I yelled. "Are you in here?"

"Yes!" Bobby said. "Me and Tuwa!"

"Oh, great!" I still couldn't see anything. But then the bubbles started moving, and I saw Bobby's hand. I grabbed it and pulled him toward me. The bubbles moved some more, and then I could see Tula. She was standing in the middle of the tub with a bubble as big as a balloon on top of her head.

" 'Happy Bubbles!' " Tula sang, like a TV commercial. " 'Leave You Clean and Leave No Ring!' " She grabbed a handful of bubbles and blew them at me. "Cool, huh, Annie?" she said.

I would have screamed, but I didn't want my parents to come running. I lifted Bobby out of the tub, dried him off, and dressed him. "Go to your room and play with your trucks," I hissed. "And Tula, you disappear!"

I guess I sounded really mad, because both of them did what I said. I spent the next thirty minutes mopping up Happy Bubbles.

By the time Monday morning came, I wondered just how much more trouble one troll could be.

CHAPTER 7

MISSING

On the way to school Monday Tula apologized for everything she'd done over the weekend. And she promised to stay out of trouble at school. "You won't even know I'm there," she said.

"Okay," I said. I wasn't sure she could keep her word, but I decided to give her a chance. I didn't have a choice, anyway. "And remember, Sam doesn't even know you exist," I told her. "So don't keep getting in a twist because he doesn't act like a real troll."

"A *twist*," Tula said. "Jason said the same thing about Kelly. But she wasn't bent into a funny shape and neither am I."

"It's an expression," I told her. "Being in a twist means being upset or bothered."

"Oh," Tula said. "Like the canine Ralph gets whenever he sees me."

"Right," I said. "Just like Ralph."

Ralph was barking at the fence again that morning. But I was in a hurry, so I told Tula not to waste time with any troll commands. She was getting an awful lot of letters mixed up, anyway. I was afraid she might tell him to attack the mailman.

When we walked into the classroom, Tula went straight to the reading corner and sat on the floor. She didn't say a word during morning math, or social studies, or spelling. She was so quiet, I kept looking to make sure she was still there. She would grin and wave at me. But she kept her lips locked.

It was late in the day when we finally went to the auditorium to practice the play. I was feeling really good. Tula wasn't causing any trouble. I knew most of my lines. Friday night was the performance, and I couldn't wait.

Just before we started the rehearsal, I realized I'd forgotten the crown. When I told Ms. Monroe, she sent Maria back to get it since I was in the first scene and we didn't want to waste time.

I was just speaking my first lines when Maria came running down the aisle.

"I couldn't find the crown!" she said. "I looked everywhere, but it's not there!"

"Uh-oh!" Jason said. "Somebody's in *big* trouble." He looked at me.

I looked at Tula. She was sitting by herself in the front row. She held her hands up and looked innocent. But I couldn't help it—I was suspicious. She'd taken the crown once. Maybe she'd taken it again.

"Did you bring it home again?" Maria asked me.

I shook my head. Kelly was walking around the stage in her black hat, practicing her cackle. I didn't want her to hear. If Tula had taken the crown, I could have it back before Kelly even knew it was missing.

But bigmouthed Jason couldn't wait to tell Kelly. "Hey, Kelly!" he said. "Guess who lost your crown?"

"Thanks a lot, Jason," I said. I looked at Kelly. "I didn't lose it," I told her.

"But it's not in the room," Maria said.

Kelly's face got red. "Oh, no!" she said. "You'd better find it, Annie!"

"I didn't lose it!"

"Well, somebody did," Kelly said. "It didn't just disappear."

Kelly gave me a dirty look and marched off.

"Somebody's in big trouble!" Jason said again.

"Will you just lock your lips, Jason?" I said. "I didn't take the crown!"

I knew *I* hadn't taken it. But I was getting more and more suspicious of Tula. I couldn't wait until I got her alone so I could tell her what I thought about troll promises.

I flubbed most of my lines during practice. Luckily, Ms. Monroe seemed to understand how upset I was. When it was over, I was the first one back to the classroom. Maria was right. The crown wasn't there. It wasn't in the reading corner, where Tula spent a lot of time, and it wasn't in my bookbag.

Ms. Monroe looked a little worried about the missing crown, but she didn't get mad. "We'll all look for it here. And Annie, you check your room at home," she said. "In the meantime, you can wear your old crown when we have practice. Okay, everybody, let's line up for dismissal."

Tula still hadn't said a word. But on the way home I said plenty to her. "Okay, Tula. Just tell me. I won't be mad. Just tell me where it is."

Tula's eyes got very wide. "The crown? Annie, I didn't take it!"

"Well, somebody did," I said. I sounded like Kelly, but I couldn't help it. "It didn't just disappear." I looked at Tula. "Or did it? Did you accidentally mix up some troll word and make it vanish? You did, didn't you?"

Tula didn't answer, but her face got as green as the grass. She was furious. She didn't say a word until we got in front of Ralph's house. When the dog came roaring over to the fence, she pointed a stubby finger at him and shouted, *"Zerbit!"*

Ralph stopped in mid-bark. Then he lay down, rolled onto one side, and didn't move.

"Now look what you did!" I cried. "You killed him!"

"Don't be hilarious," she snapped. I think she meant "ridiculous." "He's just playing dead. And it's better than the barking, isn't it?"

When we got past Ralph's yard, I turned and looked back. Ralph was sitting up and shaking his head. He was one confused dog. If I hadn't been so mad, I would have laughed.

At my house I went inside and headed straight down the hall. Bobby came running out of his room. "Tuwa?" he said.

"Not now!" I told him, I went into my room. Tula was right behind me. She hadn't even slowed down long enough to swipe a cookie.

First, I emptied my bookbag on the bed. I didn't really expect the crown to be in it, but I wanted to check again. I was right. There was no crown to be seen.

Next I headed for the desk. Tula was already

there, pulling the drawers open. We bumped elbows and heads.

"Why are *you* looking?" I asked. "If you took it, you ought to know where it is."

"I'm looking because I *didn't* take it," Tula said. She slammed a desk drawer. She went over to my dresser and started pulling out sweatshirts and socks.

"You're making a mess," I told her.

"I'm learning from you," she said.

I shoved the beanbag chair out of the way and looked behind it. No crown. Then I got down on my hands and knees and looked under the bed. One sneaker, a soccer ball, a blue stuffed rabbit, two pencils, and some dust. But no crown. I didn't even know why I was looking. I didn't bring it home, so how could it be in my room?

When I stood up, a pair of rolled-up socks hit me in the stomach. Tula was still tossing things out of my dresser.

"Why don't you just stop pretending and tell me you accidentally made it disappear?" I said.

Tula whirled around. Her face was as green as a dill pickle. "I didn't make it disappear," she said. "And if I could remember the way to get back home, I would go right now!" Then she marched across the room, jumped into the closet, and slammed the door.

I marched right after her and yanked the closet door open. Tula was sitting on my rolled-up sleeping bag. "If I get in trouble because that crown's lost," I yelled at her, "it's going to be all your fault!"

"Annie!" my mother called from the kitchen. "If you can't find something, don't blame your closet!"

CHAPTER 8

SOLVING THE RIDDLE

Tula looked at me. I looked at Tula.

We both burst out laughing at the same time.

"I'm glad you think I'm so funny, Annie," my mother called. "But I wasn't joking."

Tula and I laughed even harder. I went over to the bedroom door. "You're right, Mom!" I said in between laughs. "I shouldn't blame my closet!"

I shut the door and went back to Tula. "I shouldn't blame you, either. Sorry, Tula."

"Okay," she said. Her face was back to its normal color. She grinned at me. "You sure were twisted about it, Annie."

"I know. Maybe you should have said 'Zerbit' to me."

Tula laughed her squeaky laugh. "I would have, but you don't have a tail to wag."

"Well, anyway, I'm sorry," I said again. "I believe you about the crown now." I did, too. Tula looked so innocent, it was impossible not to believe her. "I was just upset."

"I don't blame you." Tula came out of the closet, and we started putting my socks and sweatshirts away. "You're upset because you didn't take the crown and Kelly thinks you did."

"Right. And you were mad because *you* didn't take it and I thought you did." I shut a dresser drawer. "But maybe nobody took it. Maybe it just got knocked off the shelf or something. I'll look in the classroom again tomorrow."

"Good," Tula said. "But I was thinking, Annie. Jason has a very large mouth, and he didn't stop talking about the crown at all. Do you think he took it?"

"As a joke?" I said. "He might do that. I'll have to keep an eye on him."

"No," Tula said. "*I* will keep an eye on him. And on Maria, too. After all, she went back alone to get the crown."

"Maria wouldn't take it," I said. "She doesn't joke around. And she'd be too scared of making Kelly mad."

"But maybe she accidentally broke it," Tula said. "What would she do then? Hide it so Kelly wouldn't know?"

71

"Maybe," I said.

"Well, I will look for it at lunchtime. And I will watch everyone," Tula said. "It will be a piece of pie. They'll never know they're being watched. I will be your invisible spy."

I laughed. "Where did you learn about spies?"

"On TV, where else?" Tula said. "It is a very educational invention."

For the next three days Tula played spy. She kept an eye on the other kids, especially Jason and Maria. And at lunchtime she searched every corner of the classroom. She didn't hear anybody say anything about the crown, except to bug me about where it was.

Tula and I looked and looked. But the crown stayed lost. At dress rehearsal on Friday, Kelly came over to me. "Well, Annie, have you found the crown yet?" she asked. She'd asked me the same thing every day.

"No," I said.

"You'd better," she said with a mean look on her face.

When Kelly left to practice her cackle, Sarah came over. "You should stop worrying so much," she said. "Nobody really thinks you lost the crown except Kelly. And maybe Jason," she added.

"I don't care," I said. "I still wish I could find it."

"You're a great princess without Kelly's stupid old crown," said Sarah. "And you haven't flubbed a line all week."

At the end of practice Ms. Monroe told everybody to be at school that night at six-thirty. The play started at seven-thirty. She also told me to wear my old crown, the one I'd worn at the tryouts.

"At least my old one wasn't lost," I said to Tula when we got home. I held up the old crown. "It was in my desk. It's kind of mashed."

"Maybe you can demash it," Tula said. "I'm sorry, Annie. I think Kelly's crown has truly disappeared."

"I guess so," I said. "It's a real mystery, and we don't have a single clue."

Mom let me make some sandwiches and eat them in my room at dinner so I could go over my lines one last time. After Tula and I ate, I took out my script.

"Let's just do the part where I answer the troll's riddles," I said. "Those are the only lines I have trouble with."

Tula picked up my script and cleared her throat. "What runs around a castle but never moves?" she asked.

"The castle wall," I answered.

"Next one," Tula said. "What is always in its bed but never sleeps?"

"A river," I said.

"And how do you make a troll move without touching him?"

"Take away the letter *T* and you make a troll roll."

"Excellent," Tula said. "You know them all. These are good riddles. Almost as good as the troll riddles I told you. Do you remember them?"

"Sure," I said. "How do you spell trouble with two letters? *NV*. Envy. And what do you have when you point a finger at somebody else?"

"Two fingers pointing right back at yourself!" Tula said. "Three for humans."

Three for humans, I thought. And suddenly it hit me. "Tula!" I said. "I think I know what happened to the crown!"

"What?" she asked.

"I think Kelly took it herself!"

"*Erk!*" Tula said. "Why would she do that?"

"Envy," I said. "She was jealous because I got the part of the princess. She doesn't want me to wear her crown. So maybe she took it and accused me of losing it. She's pointing a finger at me. And that means three fingers are pointing back at her!"

Tula grinned at me. "I think you have solved the mystery, Annie."

"I think so, too," I said.

Tula held up a stubby finger. "There is just one difficulty," she said. "Where did Kelly put the crown?"

"I was afraid you'd ask that," I told her. "If Kelly has it, then she probably took it home. We might have solved the mystery, but we still don't have the crown."

At six-thirty Dad dropped me off at school. He dropped Tula off, too, but he didn't know it. Then he went back home to get Mom and Bobby. "Break a leg, Annie!" he said as he drove away.

"Break a leg?" Tula said. "And I thought your father was a nice man."

"He is." I laughed. "In plays 'Break a leg' means 'Good luck.' "

Tula shook her head. "Humans," she muttered.

When we got to the auditorium, Tula went behind the curtain with me. I'd told her she could watch the play from the wings if she promised to stay out of sight.

Almost everybody was there. Sarah had on a long yellow dress. I was wearing a long blue

75

one, with a wide white sash. Jason had on black jeans and a black sweatshirt. Kelly was wearing black, too—a long witch's cape and the pointy witch's hat.

I went over to the troll's rock and put my old crown under it. Kelly came over to me.

"I see you didn't find my real one, Annie," she said.

I shook my head. I wanted to tell her I knew she'd taken it. But I wasn't completely sure. And anyway, I didn't have any proof.

Kelly frowned at me. Then she went off to the wings to practice her cackle.

Just then Ms. Monroe came up to us. "Has anyone seen Sam?" she asked. "It's almost seven. His costume is in the classroom, but he's not here yet."

Nobody had seen Sam, but nobody was worried. There was plenty of time.

At ten minutes after seven Sam still hadn't shown up. From behind the curtain, we could hear the audience coming in. I heard Bobby giggling, and I knew my parents were there. I'd been worrying so much about the crown and about Tula that I'd forgotten to get nervous. But now my heart started thumping.

At seven-fifteen Ms. Monroe was looking frantic. Sam still wasn't there.

"Did you call his house?" Maria asked.

Ms. Monroe nodded. "There was no answer."

"Maybe he's on his way," Sarah said.

"Yeah, and maybe they had a flat tire," Jason said.

"You're a big help, Jason," Sarah told him.

"It's seven-twenty," Ms. Monroe said. "The troll doesn't come on until later, so there's still time for Sam to get here. We'll just have to hope he does. Okay, everybody! It's time to take your places!"

All the kids ran to where they were supposed to be when the curtain opened.

Ms. Monroe went out in front of the curtain and made a little speech. She told the audience how we'd written the play as a class writing project. "I think you'll be very pleased and surprised at what an excellent job your children have done."

"They'll be surprised, all right," Jason said. "Especially if there's no troll."

"Be quiet!" Sarah whispered.

"And now, enjoy the play!" Ms. Monroe said. Then she went to the wings and pulled the curtain open.

My heart was pounding like crazy. Then Sarah said her first line: "Your Highness, this kingdom is getting to be a royal disaster!"

When I heard the audience laugh, I started to calm down.

The first part of the play went great. Nobody forgot any lines, and the audience clapped a lot.

Then it was time for Kelly and me to have the riddle contest with the troll. I didn't know if Sam had shown up yet. And then I saw someone crouching behind the troll's rock. Someone with pink hair. Sam had made it!

Kelly and I walked between the cardboard trees and over to the troll's rock.

"Halt!" Jason said. "Who dares disturb the mighty troll?"

"I do," I said. "I am Princess Heather. And I have come to get my crown back!"

"It's *my* crown!" Kelly the witch cackled. "I took it. I just dropped it, that's all. It belongs to me!"

Suddenly the troll leapt up and shouted, "To get your crown, you must first answer three impossible questions!"

My mouth dropped open. It was a troll, all right. Only it wasn't Sam.

It was Tula.

CHAPTER 9

SHAMAZ-SHAMAT

Everybody in the audience went "Ooh!" and "Ah!" Somebody said, "What a great makeup job!"

"Tuwa!" Bobby shouted. I heard my mother say, "Yes, Bobby, they painted tulips on the trees. Quiet, now."

"To get your crown back, you must first answer three impossible questions!" Tula shouted again. Then she jumped up and down, just like Sam. I stared at her. How had she learned the lines so fast? And she hated the way we'd written the troll, but here she was, playing the part.

I was speechless. So was Kelly.

"Who's this?" Jason whispered. "This isn't Sam."

"Psst!" Ms. Monroe hissed from the wings. She looked really confused and was staring at

79

Carol Ellis

Tula with a really confused expression, as if she'd seen her somewhere before. Finally she shook her head and said, "Go on with your lines!"

Tula put her hands on her hips. She was in Sam's costume—green pants and a matching long-sleeved T-shirt. "I will say it once more," Tula said to Kelly and me. "To get your crown back, you must first answer three impossible questions! Do you grab it now?"

I finally got my voice back. "Yes, O troll, we get it," I said. "Go ahead, ask your questions."

"But the crown is mine," Kelly said. She'd finally recovered, too. "I took it. You should give it back to me."

"You wish!" Tula said. "I found the crown when you dropped it, you clumsy witch. If you want it back, you must win the riddle game."

"Go ahead," I said again. "Ask your riddles."

Tula laughed her squeaky laugh. Then she asked the first riddle. Kelly couldn't answer it, but I could. Tula asked the second riddle. I got it right.

When I answered the third riddle, the troll was supposed to get furious because she'd lost the game.

"Take away the letter *T* and you make a troll roll!" I said.

80

Tula shouted. "Aaahh!" Then she stomped her feet and threw her arms into the air. When she did, she accidentally knocked Kelly's witch hat off. It flew across the stage and landed behind one of the big cardboard trees.

Kelly yelled, "My hat!" and ran behind the tree to get it.

I ran with her. She didn't need any help. But I needed to ask her a few questions. Because when the hat flew through the air, I saw something sparkling inside it.

I got to the hat before Kelly did and picked it up. Stuck inside, as far up as it would go, was Kelly's crown.

"I was right!" I whispered. "You took it!"

"That stupid troll!" Kelly said. "It's all his fault. Or hers. Who *is* that, anyway?"

"Never mind," I said. "You were jealous, weren't you? That's why you took it," I said.

"No ... I ..." Kelly looked me straight in the eye. "Okay, yes! *I* wanted to be the princess!" she said. "No one was supposed to wear the crown but me!"

"Girls!" Ms. Monroe said in a loud whisper. "Go on with the play!"

Jason was waving his hands at Kelly and me. Tula was still stomping her feet and yelling because she had to give the crown back. "I'm ruined!" she shouted. "I'll never be the same troll again!" She was doing a great job playing the part—she sounded even louder and meaner than Sam!

I had some more questions for Kelly, but they would have to wait. I ran back over to Tula. Kelly was right behind me. "I have come for my crown," I announced to Tula.

"It's about time," Jason whispered.

Tula lifted up the rock. Before she could take out my old crown, Kelly moved over next to her. She stooped down so nobody could see and took her crown out of her hat. Then she gave it to Tula.

"Erk!" Tula said. She almost grinned at me, but she stopped herself in time. "I am ruined!" she shouted again. Then she handed me Kelly's crown and ran off into the wings.

I put the sparkly crown on my head. "Behold!" I cried. "My crown has been returned to me. Our kingdom will be grumpy no more!"

Everybody in the princess's kingdom cheered. The audience clapped. And Ms. Monroe closed the curtain.

After the play we all went to our classroom to take our costumes off and wait for our parents. Everybody was talking about the troll.

"Who was it?" Jason asked. "I know it wasn't Sam."

"It wasn't me," Sarah said. "But whoever it was was really good."

"And really strange," said Jason.

"I'll tell you something that's strange," Maria said. "Look at my script." She held it up. Some of the pages were almost completely gone. And the little pieces that were left had teeth marks on them. Now I knew how Tula had learned her lines so fast. She'd eaten them! "Maybe it was the ghost who ate my script and played the troll," Maria said.

"Get real," Jason told her. "A mouse probably ate your script. And the troll was one of us. I'm going to find out who." He started walking around the room, asking everybody questions.

I didn't see Tula at all. I put my blue dress in the costume box and was just going to look for her when Kelly came in from the hall. She looked unhappy. I went over to talk to her.

"I don't get it," I said. "Why'd you stick the crown in your hat? Why didn't you just take it home?"

"Because we weren't allowed to take our costumes home, remember?" Kelly answered. She took off the long black robe she had over her clothes. "I wanted to hide it, so I got in early one morning. I was going to put it in my bookbag, but I heard somebody coming. So I stuffed it in my witch hat real fast."

"And you blamed me for losing it," I said. "All because you were jealous."

"I was jealous, but that's not the only reason I took the crown back," she said. She looked ashamed. "See, I never told my mother that I brought it here in the first place. I thought for sure I'd get the part of the princess, and *then* I'd ask her if I could use it."

"Oh, now I get it," I said. "If your mother saw it onstage, you'd be in *big* trouble."

Kelly nodded. "And I was right. My mom recognized her tiara tonight, and she just gave me a long lecture. I wouldn't have let you wear it, but I was afraid you'd tell Ms. Monroe on me." She held out her hand. "Can I have it back now?"

I took the crown off my head and gave it to her. "Thanks," Kelly mumbled.

Just then Ms. Monroe came in. "I finally got an answer at Sam's home," she said. "You were right, Jason. They got stuck in traffic and then they had a flat tire and couldn't get to a phone. They were on the way back from the doctor—Sam has the chicken pox."

Jason started scratching his arms. "I'm feeling very itchy all of a sudden. I think I might have to miss school next week."

"Forget it, Jason," Sarah told him. "You had chicken pox in first grade, remember?"

"Well, at least we had a troll to take Sam's place." Ms. Monroe frowned. "I'm sure I've seen her somewhere before. Or him. I just can't remember where," she said. She looked puzzled. Finally she laughed. "Oh, I know!" she said. "It was one of you, wasn't it? Now, which one was it?"

Nobody answered.

"All right, don't tell me," she said, laughing again. "I'll find out!"

I smiled to myself. I knew she never would.

Sarah came home with me to spend the night. By the time we left school, I still hadn't found Tula. I was a little worried. But when Sarah and I went into my room, I noticed that the closet door wasn't closed all the way. Tula must be waiting in there, I thought.

Sarah flopped into my beanbag chair and opened the bag of popcorn we'd picked up in the kitchen. "The play turned out great, didn't it?" she said. "The mystery troll was the best."

"The troll was fantastic." I said it real loud to make sure Tula could hear me.

"So were you," Sarah said. "And Kelly's crown looked perfect. I can't believe all her mother did was lecture her about taking it." I had told Sarah about my conversation with

Kelly, of course. "My mother would have grounded me for life."

"Mine, too," I said. I looked at the closet. Now was the time to introduce Sarah and Tula, I decided.

I walked over to the closet. "Come here," I said to Sarah. "I have something to show you."

Sarah got out of the chair and walked over to me. "What?" she said.

"A surprise," I told her. "You might not believe it at first. But it's true. Close your eyes."

Sarah giggled and closed her eyes. I opened the closet door.

Tula wasn't there.

"Can I look now?" Sarah said.

"Just a second." I stepped into the closet. There was something different about it. It was clean. All the shoes were lined up on one side. The stuffed animals were in a neat row on the other. Toys and books and magazines were back on the shelves. My sleeping bag was rolled up, and there was a piece of paper on top of it.

"Come on, Annie!" Sarah opened her eyes and looked. "Hey, you cleaned out your closet. You're right, I don't believe it." She laughed. "This popcorn's making me awfully thirsty. Can I go get us something to drink?"

"Sure," I said. When Sarah had gone, I

picked up the piece of paper. It was a note from Tula.

"Dear Annie,

"You were great in the play! I am glad you got to wear the real crown. You really did solve the mystery.

"While I was pretending to be your wicked troll, it suddenly smacked me—it was time to go home! I miss all my *real* troll friends. If I'm not here when you come back, then I finally got the magic right!

Shamaz-Shamat,
Tula!

"P.S. I have had an awesomely weird time in your world. If I'm not in a mountain of trouble for sneaking out, I'll come back and see you again."

"I'll be waiting, Tula," I whispered. I stuffed the note under my mattress. Sarah would have to wait until the next time to meet the troll in my closet.

ABOUT THE AUTHOR
AND ILLUSTRATOR

CAROL ELLIS is the author of over twenty books for young readers, including the best-selling *Camp Fear*, *The Window*, and *The Stepdaughter*. Carol Ellis lives in New York with her husband and son.

PAT PORTER has illustrated over twenty-five children's books, including *Slime Time*, *Luke's Bully*, and the notable, *Blue Tree Red Sky*, by Norma Klein. She has lived in New York for over 30 years.